This special
edition of
THE
FOUR THOUSAND,
THE
EIGHT HUNDRED
is limited to
1000 numbered copies.

This is copy __691__ .

THE
FOUR THOUSAND,
THE
EIGHT HUNDRED

THE
FOUR THOUSAND,
THE
EIGHT HUNDRED

GREG EGAN

SUBTERRANEAN PRESS 2016

First Edition

ISBN
978-1-59606-791-2

Subterranean Press
PO Box 190106
Burton, MI 48519

subterraneanpress.com

1

CAMILLE peered out from her cocoon into the star-strewn blackness, waiting for the moment of terror to come and grant her a modicum of peace. Every minute she spent awake only wasted her resources and added to the risk that her heat signature would be detected, but she didn't dare begin hibernation until she knew for sure that she was well-enough secured to survive at least one collision. If she was shaken loose at the very first impact—still awake, still in sight of Vesta—she might have a chance to make it home. Any time after that, it would be fatal.

The cocoon was only a few centimetres wider than her suit in any direction, and its thick acrylic walls undermined the crisp transparency of her face plate, leaving her with a dull, distorted view. Elastic restraints kept her from rattling around inside her plastic coffin, but since it was glued smack on the rotational pole of the ten-metre slab of basalt—whose spin was so stately that her mind wandered every time she tried to track the turning of the stars—her own fidgeting far outweighed any centrifugal force. She'd stopped responding to every maddening itch, but she was afraid of keeping her legs too still lest she find herself with a painful cramp that she'd have no room to deal with.

She turned her head to the left and forced her body to the right against the tug of the restraints, until she could just make out part of Vesta below her, a lopsided crescent almost bisected by the slab's horizon. *How many more of her friends would die, before she saw this world again?* She shaped her lips and blew across her face to dislodge the tears.

Her neck began to ache, so she twisted it in the opposite direction to let the muscles recover. To her right, the silhouette of a solar collector carved a black ellipse out of the stars. Camille caught a glint against this dark background, probably sunlight reflecting off another slab of cargo, but she couldn't tell if it was export or import; the same white polymer sheaths covered Vestan rock and Cererian ice. Each world had too much of one and too little of the other, so for generations they'd been swapping tonne for tonne, turning each other's dross into riches. But now here she was spoiling the symmetry, hitching a ride on the river of stone, an export no one had ordered or authorised.

Vertigo gripped her, then subsided, leaving her stomach clenched and a ringing in her ears. She turned her gaze back to Vesta and saw her home world drifting serenely along the edge of the slab. The collision she'd been dreading had come and gone, rendered so smooth by the rebounding of the sheaths that this crash of boulders had delivered no greater jolt to her body than a fiercely returned serve in a game of squash. But however gentle the encounter had seemed, the rock she was riding had been struck head-on by an equally massive block of ice, and like the pieces in a cosmic Newton's cradle the two had had no choice but to exchange their states of motion: the ice now took her place in the parking orbit, while she, very slowly, was on her way to Ceres.

Camille managed a sob of relief. The collisions yet to come would be with helper rocks, ferrying momentum from the ever more distant river of ice, but the effects should be no rougher. Gustave's handiwork had passed the test.

Every breath was a luxury now. Camille spoke to the cocoon's controller and told it to begin its task.

She relaxed and let the restraints pull her limbs clear of the upper wall, which abruptly turned opaque and plunged her into darkness. The vacuum between her suit and this carapace would allow its outer surface to cool far below her hibernation temperature, while the rock behind her back was massive enough to absorb the trickle of her residual body heat and barely show it.

When the venous tap in her elbow opened, the outflow was almost imperceptible; the shock came when the same fluid was returned to her, chilled. Five degrees centigrade hadn't sounded so bad when she'd fitted the pump; with no ice crystals to burst her cell walls, the drug cocktail didn't even need antifreeze. But her shivering flesh didn't understand the biomedical pros and cons: she just felt as if she had suffered a wound so sharp and deep that it put an end to any distinction between her body's interior and the world beyond, allowing this flood of icy water to engulf her from within.

"Stay safe," she murmured. Her mother's words to her, her own to her mother. Camille repeated them until her lips went numb. Five years before, she'd treated a young joyrider whose suit had been torn open all the way along one arm, allowing the rocks on Vesta's surface to touch his naked skin and turn his flesh necrotic with cold. And now here she was, pinned to a heat sink more than sufficient to suck every trace of living warmth out of her and leave nothing but a sack of purplish-black sherbet. She'd checked the pump and the drugs herself, but it wouldn't matter what was flowing through her veins if the cocoon's thermostat went awry and she dropped all the way to the ambient temperature.

Gustave had promised that she'd be euphoric as her consciousness slipped away, but he would have told her anything to keep her from backing out. What finally took the edge off her panic was simply a deadening of her senses, an absence of signals from her body much like the onset of ordinary sleep.

As the darkness behind her eyes deepened, Camille looked down from on high and pictured the journey to come: her slow spiral out to Ceres, the hundred gentle nudges, the thousand days slipping by in silence. Her fear was gone; all she felt now was grief and shame. Her escape was a *fait accompli*, but the fight would go on without her.

2

"**WE** have a rider," Anna's Assistant declared.

"Show me." Anna accepted the overlay and stared at the infrared image of the cargo sheath. The green-tinged blotch stood out clearly against the square of blue—but the legend putting numbers to hues showed that the difference in temperature between the two was only a fraction of a degree.

"How long to recovery?" she asked.

"We should be able to detach the life support structure and get it to an airlock within forty-five minutes. I've notified the medical team."

Anna switched views to a traffic control map of the port. The tug that had imaged the rider was now ferrying the cube of basalt down to a powered orbit that would allow it to hover just a few hundred metres above the surface. Two specialised extraction robots were already waiting outside the nearest airlock, ready to rise up and do their work. The tugs' automated checks were usually reliable, but Anna's skin crawled at the thought of what might have happened if the rider had been missed. The pods were meant to activate radio beacons and start heating up to human-friendly temperatures once they were close to their destination, but before it was understood that they sometimes failed to do that, three riders had been crushed to death by machinery meant for handling much more robust cargo.

Anna rearranged herself restlessly in her hammock, then made a decision and pulled herself free. "I'm going to meet the medical team by the airlock," she told her Assistant as she started down the corridor, dragging herself along the guide rope until she could build up enough velocity to glide. The protocol did not require her presence, but she was responsible for the recovery, and it did not feel right to loll around her office while this person's life was still in the balance.

The grey stone walls flew past her: Vestan rock, all of it. People dawdled in the corridor, chatting, scowling at her unseemly haste. Anna grabbed the rope to correct her downwards drift and replenish her speed. "How's the extraction going?" she asked her Assistant.

"The robots are *in situ*, but still assessing the structure."

"What about the medical team?"

"They should be at the airlock in about ten minutes."

When Anna arrived, the team was setting up their equipment. Her Assistant made the introductions, putting names to the three faces; Anna merely nodded a greeting.

"Your first rider?" Pyotr asked, a little amused that the port's director had chosen to join him and his colleagues.

"Yes." Anna didn't think she owed him an explanation, but she wanted to make it clear that she was here to learn, not to interfere. "Six days into the job, there are still a lot of firsts."

"This is routine now," Pyotr assured her. "And so long as we spot the pods, ice-cream scoops tend to do better than wrigglers." Anna hadn't come across this terminology before, but she resisted the urge to express an opinion on it. "I've been telling people to try to get the word back to Vesta about that," Pyotr added, with a note of frustration. "Everything about the process is a thousand times safer in a hospital bed than it is in deep space. They should just start up the beacon and leave the rest to us."

"It's a long pipeline," Anna replied. Even if the advice was heeded, it would take years to have any effect on the state of new arrivals. But it would also take a lot of faith in your rescuers, to relinquish the one trace of autonomy that remained when you consigned yourself to the journey.

The robots began detaching the pod. Anna watched the overlays, sharing the machines' vision as one sliced through the cargo sheath and the other gripped the opaque cylinder. Synthetic imagery blossomed over the ordinary multispectral visuals, as ultrasound echoes built up a map of stresses in the pod walls and MRI tomography revealed the intact pressure suit and the living form within. Anna's attention skated over most of the data screed, but the layperson's summaries of the blood proteins suggested that the rider had suffered no life support glitches or adverse health events.

The robot holding the pod rose up from the cargo block, but even in transit it kept working: a bright red gash grew lengthwise along the cylinder, the heat signature of a laser cutting through the wall. By the time Anna heard the faint thump of arrival above her and the hum of the airlock's outer door opening, the outline of a rectangular aperture was all but complete.

The robot lowered the pod gently into the airlock and retreated. Anna dismissed the overlays and looked across the vestibule as Pyotr, Alex and Elena gathered around the inner door. Air sighed into the vacuum of the lock, a long, slow exhalation.

When the door slid open Alex stepped inside and manoeuvred the pod out, bear-hugging it from behind. Anchored to the floor with geckoed soles, he held the pod still while Pyotr cut through the final centimetre that was keeping the pane of white plastic in place, then lifted it away with a suction pad. Anna grabbed a guide rope and raised herself up to a better vantage point.

Elena attached a probe to the exterior of the rider's suit, then after about a minute reached an assessment and began unscrewing the bolts that held the helmet in place.

Between the three busy figures obscuring the view, Anna caught glimpses of a young man's face. The closed eyes appeared gluey; there was no visible exudation, but the lids were oddly wrinkled in a way that ought not have persisted had they been free to smooth themselves out. The man's hollow cheeks bore what looked like two or three days' worth of dark stubble, which seemed eerier than the Rip Van Winkle beard that such a journey should have allowed. The drugs and the cold had slowed his metabolism to the point where an intravenous recycler with a single fuel cell and a kilogram of top-up supplies had been enough to keep him alive for three years—but though he might not have taken a breath since Vesta, time hadn't stopped for him entirely.

Anna felt a pang of unease at her voyeurism; she let herself drop towards the floor and turned her gaze aside. After a few minutes, the team extracted the man from the pod and laid him on the life-support gurney they'd brought. He was still in his suit, but one sleeve had been cut off. Elena attached a new tube to the port strapped to her patient's elbow, and a pump inside the gurney began to whir.

Pyotr approached Anna. "It looks as if he's going to be fine. His dosimeter shows that he stayed well-shielded, and there's no sign of clots or ischaemia. But we'll get him to the hospital and do a full investigation."

"How long until he wakes?"

"A couple of days. It's safer to take it slowly."

"Right." She reached out and shook his hand. "Thank you."

Pyotr smiled. "You're welcome, Madam Director."

Anna raised a hand in farewell to the rest of the team, then turned and left them to their work. Perhaps she'd deserved Pyotr's gentle mockery: her presence had contributed nothing. But until the day came when the port was placed entirely in the hands of machines, she was the token human in the loop. She was paying a third of her income for the privilege; if she wasn't going to take the job seriously there was no point doing it at all.

3

"FREELOADER," someone muttered. Not loudly, but they'd leant close enough to Camille's ear to leave her in no doubt that the insult was meant for her.

She looked around the crowd of students squeezing their way out of the lecture theatre. One man, ahead of her in the throng, glanced back at her and met her gaze disdainfully before turning away.

"What did you call me?" she asked, raising her voice to be heard over the chatter, but not enough to make a scene. The man offered no reply, and after a moment he pushed his way forward out of sight.

Olivier touched her elbow. "What's wrong?"

"Did you hear what he said?"

"No."

Camille repeated the word. Just saying it made her uncomfortable. Olivier grimaced with disdain. "Forget it."

"It's Denison's term," she replied. "And now people are using it."

"Denison's a crackpot. No one takes him seriously."

"Except the ones who do." Camille's skin went cold. "I've never spoken to that man in my life! How does he know who my great-great-grandparents were?"

Olivier was silent.

"How?" Camille pressed him. If he'd had no idea, he would have said so immediately.

"Let's get some food," he suggested.

In the cafeteria, Olivier showed her the aug, putting up the description in a shared overlay. "It estimates someone's degree of relatedness to each founder, based on facial metrics. But it's been around for years; it's got nothing to do with Denison."

Camille scrolled through to the available add-ons. "Except now you can tweak it to label anyone in sight who has more than fifty percent of their ancestors from the Sivadier syndicate."

Olivier spread his hands. "Yes. And there are augs that label anyone in sight who matches the user's aesthetic predilections—lest a potential object of desire slip past in a moment of inattention. If you're going to judge the whole of Vesta by the crassest augs on offer, you might as well slit your wrists right now."

Camille was unswayed. "Have you read *The New Dispensation*?"

"I skimmed it," Olivier confessed. "It was so stupid that I lost patience halfway through."

Camille had seen eccentric rants on all sorts of issues blaze into prominence and then fade back to obscurity, but six months on, Denison's manifesto still hadn't gone the way of most viral pap. When Vesta had been colonised, the founders had agreed that all of their offspring would share equally in the wealth that came from the enterprise. But while the other syndicates had contributed tangible assets—the ships that carried the colonists, the robots that dug the first settlements and mines—the Sivadiers had brought expertise and intellectual property. The other founders had apparently valued these things highly enough to welcome their colleagues on equal terms, but in Denison's version of history it was a partnership built on extortion. How could it be fair that Isabelle Sivadier and her cronies had wheedled their way into the deal with nothing but their rent-seeking stranglehold on certain mining techniques, while everyone else had paid their share in the honest currency of tonnes conveyed to orbit?

"Do you remember the last line?" she asked.

Olivier shook his head.

"'It's time for the Sivadiers to repay their debt. With interest.'"

"And he's going to make this happen...how?" Olivier put on his best tough-guy scowl. "Hey Denison: you and whose army?"

"You and whose accountants," Camille corrected him.

He laughed. "Yeah." He leant across the table and kissed her.

The table buzzed in complaint until Olivier took his elbows away so the serving hatch could open; their meals rose up, steaming and aromatic. As Camille slid her plate closer, she thought: No one's going to tear up the contract that's defined this world for more than a century. And no one's going to take the food out of my mouth because I belong to the wrong family.

4

ON their way to the hospital, Anna insisted that they make a detour to the fruit market.

"You don't think they're feeding him properly?" Chloe joked.

"It's just a gesture," Anna replied, rummaging through a stack of plums. Her Assistant started annotating each fruit with nutritional estimates, but Anna waved the data away. What mattered was the shape and colour, and she could judge those qualities herself.

"He's not really *ill*," Chloe observed, as if that had some bearing on the relevance of the gift. "Every rider goes through the same stages. It's a normal transition."

"I see. So three years on an intravenous drip in lieu of food and air is no big deal: it's as natural as puberty or menopause."

Chloe persisted. "The Vestans call those life-support pods 'cocoons'. So they must think of the process as a kind of metamorphosis."

"You brought me flowers when I had Sasha," Anna recalled. "Was I ill?"

"No."

Anna chose two plums, two apples and two mandarins. It was probably too much to eat, but anything less would have looked miserly. "Buy these," she told her Assistant. She put the fruit in her backpack and bounded away from the stall, in her haste almost missing the guide rope she'd been aiming for. Chloe caught up with her, tumbling elegantly in midair before taking a handhold beside her.

As they entered the hospital, Anna began to have second thoughts. Her Assistant had had no trouble booking the visit, so both the rider himself and the doctors treating him must have agreed to it, but what if she was intruding? Most new arrivals had plenty of contacts among the established Vestan émigrés, and there were professional social workers to ease the path into Cererian society for the few who didn't. Why would this man want some random bureaucrat turning up for no reason, carrying enough vegetable fibre to tear a new hole in his atrophied colon?

They turned off the corridor into the ward. Most of the beds had their privacy curtains in place, but they didn't need to go far to see where their company was expected.

"Anna?" The rider was propped up on a stack of pillows, beaming at her. Her Assistant captioned his face as "Olivier Druillet", but an icon beside the name warned her that some glitch had prevented a reciprocal annotation.

"That's right," Anna replied—in French, hoping that that wasn't condescending. For a second she was flustered by the system's failure to handle all the niceties, but then she got her bearings and introduced Chloe. She geckoed her soles and approached the bed on foot, preparing to offer her hand, but then Olivier leant forward and embraced her.

"Thank you for coming," he said, accepting her choice of language.

"It's my pleasure," Anna replied. Chloe kept her distance, smiling amiably. "How are you feeling?"

"Still a little groggy, but they tell me that's normal." He looked painfully gaunt, but it had only been five days since he'd been plucked from the pod.

Anna hesitated, then took the fruit out of her backpack. Olivier thanked her and slipped it into a net sack beside the bed.

"Do you have friends on Ceres?" Chloe asked.

"Of course. They were here this morning." His smile remained fixed but the joy drained away behind it. "Catching me up on things."

Anna didn't pursue the subject. The news from Vesta hadn't been good for a long time, and three years' worth in one hit would be a lot to cope with.

"So you're the port's director?" he asked.

"Yes."

"That means it's you who let me into Ceres?"

Anna laughed. "I suppose it is, officially. But I can't claim much credit for that; I wouldn't have kept the job for long if I'd strapped you to the next ice block instead."

Olivier turned to Chloe. "May I ask what you do?"

"Nothing I have to pay for," Chloe replied.

"Fair enough."

"How long will they keep you here?" Anna asked.

"A couple more days."

"Do you have somewhere to stay?"

Olivier nodded. "There's a friend I can share with."

"The housing queue's not bad right now," Anna assured him. "You'll have a place of your own in a couple of months."

"Thank you." He looked uncomfortable, as if this prospect were some kind of embarrassing extravagance. Anna had heard that the "Sivadiers" had been denied new accommodation on Vesta for years. She thought of quipping that the building material would be mostly from his home world anyway, but then she was afraid that this might sound flippant.

Chloe said, "That's just the way things work here. It's a policy, not a gift."

"Then I thank you for your policy," Olivier replied.

"We should let you rest," Anna decided. "I don't think your comms are sorted yet, but you can look me up if you want to get in touch."

Olivier offered her his hand. "It was good to meet you both."

5

"THIS is a mistake." Camille stared at the words in the overlay in front of her, wondering if they could be a hoax. But the message had been signed with Leon's private key—and if that had been breached, he would have kicked up a mighty public fuss.

She turned to her mother. "No one will vote for this, whoever the proposer is."

Her mother said, "Some people think it will quiet things down. Especially because of who the proposer is."

Camille felt her face flush with anger. "So in the face of extortion, the great plan is...*appeasement?*"

"A ten percent cut. What's that?" Her mother gestured to take in the worldly goods around them: the cabinet with its crockery, the cooking pots, the larder. "It would hardly plunge us into poverty."

"But what's next? They charge an extra ten percent for our jobs? Or they confine us to ten percent of the city?"

"No one's going to let your training go to waste."

Camille scowled. "It doesn't matter whether I can work or not. It's about the way we're all treated." This "we" that she'd never even wanted. And the last person she felt the slightest trace of solidarity with right now was Leon Sivadier, whatever ridiculous kind of cousin-esque thing he was to her. The reason there was no name for such distant relatives was because sane people would have no interest in distinguishing them from anyone else.

"Once we're paying off the debt, that's it, it's over." Her mother fidgeted with the sleeve of her blouse. "What more can anyone ask for?"

"There is no *debt*," Camille replied. "If Denison told you that the Tooth Fairy was a Sivadier, and he's forwarding the bill for her hip replacement in 1829, would you pay that too?"

Her mother looked at her squarely. "I don't feel safe anymore. In the markets, people insult me to my face. Everywhere I go now, I'm looking over my shoulder. I'm tired of it. I just want this resolved."

Camille said, "If anyone actually assaulted you, you know how many feeds they'd need to block, how many logs they'd need to wipe to get away with it? And what kind of person would even *want* to lay a hand on you because of some historical-revisionist business dispute?"

"The kind who thinks they're not getting satisfaction through the ordinary procedures of business."

"The adjudicators said there was no case." Camille's jaw tightened with frustration. "How is that our fault? Not one 'Sivadier' among them—and they all ruled that the plaintiffs were grasping at air."

Her mother said, "We're outnumbered ten to one. If the majority believe that they're the victims of injustice, it doesn't matter what the adjudicators say."

"The majority don't believe that." Every one of Camille's friends had expressed their disgust at the New Dispensation Movement. She wasn't going to be intimidated by a few cowards who shouted abuse when their augs flagged a safe target.

"Then they'll vote down the proposition," her mother said, "and perhaps that will be enough to clear the air."

"Hmm." Maybe that was what Leon was hoping for. Camille reconsidered her position. Holding the ballot still seemed like a humiliating endorsement of Denison's libel, but by putting the matter in the hands of ordinary Vestans, they had a chance to expose the NDM as extremists with no real support—a tiny group of vexatious litigants, powered by nothing but their own limitless sense of entitlement.

"I can't stop this going ahead," Camille conceded. "But if you vote yes, I'll have to disown you." She'd meant the last part to sound like a joke, but it didn't quite emerge that way.

"It's none of your business how I vote," her mother replied.

Camille said, "Just think about what this would mean! Do you really want people to start choosing *who they have children with* in order to spare them the Sivadier Tax?"

Her mother shook her head dismissively. "All I want is for you to be safe."

☉

Camille put her name in the pool to speak in one of the debates on the proposition, but she didn't even make it into the live audience. She watched the first event in Olivier's apartment; they sat on the couch, sharing an overlay.

"Throughout history, marauding armies on Earth looted the cultural treasures of nations and seized the private assets of their enemies. But we all celebrate those rare cases where justice was done in the end, and the inheritors of this ill-gotten bounty were forced to return it to its rightful owners, or pay appropriate reparations." Sandrine Marquet spoke with calm conviction. If Camille had missed the introduction and blanked the subsequent identifying captions, she would have been nodding along right now at the sheer reasonableness of the woman's arguments. No one could deny that all manner of temporal and spiritual authorities had, over the ages, given their blessing to countless acts of theft, annexation and enslavement. But however many generations passed before the plunderers were finally recognised as such, one principle was clear: there was no moral alibi to be found by appealing to the laws of the day.

"If 'intellectual property' is anathema to us now," Marquet argued, "how absurd and distasteful it would be to make some kind of culturally relativistic excuse for the way this concept was used by the Sivadiers to bully their way into the Vestan project. Yes, they were parties to a contract that was entered into by mutual consent. But if the entire legal framework of the time was corrupt—supporting the buying and selling of ideas that were the birthright of all humankind—what chance was there for justice, back then?"

By the time the broadcast paused for an intermission, Olivier was optimistic. "There's some stirring rhetoric there, all right, but I think the vagueness undermines it. And it's not as if there's nothing concrete from that era they could raise, if they wanted to: there are studies showing that overpriced tests for patented oncogenes actually led to people dying."

"But precision invites distinctions," Camille replied. "Mining tech and medical tech are too hard to blur together."

"As opposed to mining tech and war crimes?"

"That's the genius of it," Camille decided. "There is no real comparison; it's just inviting people to associate the two. But if you try to unpick that association, you end up sounding obtusely literal-minded."

The speaker for the negative, David Delille, started by presenting his ancestry records, to prove that he would not be subject to the tax himself. Perhaps it gave him a warm inner glow to announce that he was acting purely out of principle, but Camille just felt dismayed by the attempt to link credibility with *pedigree*.

In his rebuttal, Delille sought to out-Marquet Marquet: "I agree that we've moved on from the appalling moral failures of our ancestors—which is why this proposed act of collective punishment must be rejected. History also records the cases of victors extracting unjust reparations. Do we want to be judged as we now judge them: petty, vindictive, avaricious, and ultimately self-defeating?"

Camille pressed her face into a cushion to keep herself from screaming. All of this wallowing in Nuremberg and Versailles sounded terribly high-minded, but it left precious little time to discuss the actual situation.

When the whole dispiriting thing was over, Olivier suggested that she post a response. He knew she'd made notes when she'd still hoped to get a spot in one of the debates herself.

"I'm not prepared," she replied. "And no one watches those things unless they show up straight away."

"We still have a window," he said. "Come on, I'll help you."

They put something together in half an hour, and it didn't look too bad. They were far from the first wave, but interest in the debate persisted, and after a couple of hours people started viewing her contribution.

"Now you're famous," Olivier joked, as the count entered triple digits.

"Famous for declaring that patents on asteroid mining did not delay the eradication of malaria. For my next trick, maybe I should take on the nexus between cat ownership and human sacrifice." She turned to Olivier. "Tell me this is all a bad dream."

"Wait until we reach the part where I'm standing at the edge of Rheasilvia, naked."

"I'm serious."

"You seriously think you're dreaming?"

"I seriously need to hear that this can't happen."

Olivier winced. "'Can't' is such a strong word. And my record of predictions hasn't been too strong so far."

"So what will we do if the vote gets through?"

He took the cushion from her hands and held it against his chin. "Try slapping each other until we wake."

☾

On the day of the vote, Camille had a late shift in the emergency clinic. It started out even quieter than usual, and she passed the time reviewing case notes. She set her reading aug to clear the view at the slightest hint of activity around her, but hours crept by without interruption until she shut off the overlay herself to rest, staring down the empty corridor.

A young woman approached, clutching her stomach, bent over, wincing with pain. Camille strode forward to meet her, imager in hand. She hated having to gecko when she was in a hurry, but she'd hate it even more if she misjudged a leap and head-butted a patient with a burst appendix.

"Can you tell me what happened?"

The woman shook her head, groaning.

"When did the pain start?"

Still no reply.

"Can you take your hands away so I can do a scan?"

The woman looked up at Camille. "No."

"Why not?"

"You haven't earned the right to lay a finger on me. I'll try another clinic."

"I'm sorry?" Camille was about to explain that she could bring in a senior colleague to consult by telepresence at a moment's notice, when her reluctant patient made the situation clear.

"You heard me, freeloader." The woman turned and shuffled away, keeping up a desultory mime of discomfort for a few metres before snickering and breaking into a normal stride.

Camille had trained herself long ago not to swear at patients who puked on her. That discipline kept her silent as she walked back to her post.

The shift turned out to be the busiest she'd faced all year. People came limping, moaning, screaming. Some were supported by able-bodied friends, some were alone. Others showed up in packs, taking their cues from each other's symptoms—pretending to be the casualties of a single bad batch of intoxicants.

Camille dealt with them all in good faith, taking each charade as far as it needed to be taken. Most of the hoaxers reached a point early in her assessment when they made a show of scrutinising her face, detecting her ancestry and recoiling in disdain. Only a few kept up the bad acting after she'd determined that there was nothing wrong with them—and when she offered them a second opinion, they inevitably declined and retreated.

Nuisance flash mobs had long been the weapon of choice of aggrieved, inarticulate adolescents with a pack-hunting mentality. She did not feel physically threatened; the security robot in the corner of the clinic had proved itself effective enough when patients with genuinely altered mental states had tried to grope, stab or choke her. But while she kept up her veneer of professionalism, a part of her began to fantasise about grabbing one of these smirking buffoons by the shoulders and screaming in their face, "What is your problem? My ancestors made a living from their wits. Why should I beg for your forgiveness for that, when it's clear that your own were witless?"

Twenty minutes before the end of the shift, a group of fourteen people traipsed into the clinic, all of them young, most of them men. They were babbling incoherently, pulling faces, laughing and weeping. Camille chose one to start with, and when he gave no meaningful response to her questions she took him into the examination cubicle and drew the curtain.

While he sat in the harness, his head lolling and his gaze sweeping around at random, his companions started insinuating their way into the cubicle. Camille brought up an overlay from the robot; it was already restraining four people, the most its arms could hold, but no one was being aggressive enough to warrant greater force or chemical sedation.

Camille swung around to face the intruders. "Get out of here!" she said sharply. "I'm trying to help your friend."

The woman nearest to her stared back uncomprehendingly. Camille was trembling. No one had touched her, or threatened her—and a part of her was already second-guessing the whole thing, wondering if she'd look weak and incompetent if she summoned assistance to help her deal with these barely animated rag dolls.

The small luminous square in the corner of her vision blinked out; her link to the robot was gone. She tried to re-establish it, but all her comms were down. The clinic had a dozen security cameras, but she didn't know if they used radio or optical fibres.

Behind her, the man in the harness spoke. "I hope we're not making too much trouble. We were celebrating, and it seems to have got out of hand." His words were perfectly clear now.

Camille turned to him. "If there's nothing wrong with you, why don't you fuck off?"

"Gladly." He clambered out of the harness and stood beside her, soles clinging to the floor. "But aren't you going to ask what we were celebrating?"

Camille didn't reply. The man stared back at her for a few seconds, then smiled and led his companions out of the cubicle.

Camille waited until they were gone to check her link; it was working again. She opened a news feed and brought up the results. Voting was over, and the tax on the Sivadiers had been accepted by a majority of fifty-two percent.

She went into the toilets and sat down in a cubicle; it was the only way she could escape the cameras herself. Then she cradled her head in her arms and wept with rage.

6

"YOUR partner couldn't make it?" Olivier asked Anna.

"This isn't her kind of thing." Chloe had offered no excuse or apology, and Anna didn't feel inclined to invent one.

Olivier led her into the crowded apartment. Percussive music with an unfamiliar rhythm was playing softly, almost lost beneath the voices of the guests, and there was a heady aroma of frying spices escaping from the kitchen. When her host began making introductions Anna wondered if she should gently remind him that everyone's name was visible to her—but he could hardly be unaware of that, and if he wished to provide her with these verbal précis it would be rude to interrupt.

"Laurent and I knew each other for years, back on Vesta," Olivier explained, of the apartment's owner. "I doubt I would have made it through medical school if he hadn't brought out the competitive streak in me."

Laurent put a brotherly arm across Olivier's shoulders. "I'm just glad to see him here, in safety. And Camille, before too long."

Olivier's smile faltered. "That's more than a year away."

"The time will pass quickly," Laurent insisted. "Before you know it, she'll be standing on the spot where you are now."

Olivier didn't seem to take much comfort from this hyperbole. Anna said, "It looks like you have your strength back. You're walking around as if you just stepped off the ferry."

"The muscles don't get much of a chance to atrophy," Olivier explained. "If you measure the journey time biologically, it's only equivalent to a few days' bed rest."

"We do have stronger gravity, though."

"Sixteen percent?" He looked down at his still absurdly slender frame. "I think I've compensated for that in other ways."

The doorbell rang, and Olivier excused himself.

"Your friend Camille is…en route?" Anna asked Laurent.

"Yes. She left about two years ago."

"I don't know how anyone can do that," Anna confessed. "I don't even like going up to the surface."

"You'd have no choice," Laurent replied amiably.

Anna had no wish to offend him, but she wasn't sure that this was literally true. "If you were captured, how bad would it be?"

"The sentence for insurrection is life in prison. And that's the best outcome. People die while they're being arrested, all the time."

"But it can't go on like that forever," she protested. "There must be some way to settle the whole dispute."

"There must," Laurent agreed. "But we can't accept anything less than the restoration of equality, and right now there's no prospect of that."

As Olivier rejoined them, Anna noticed that half a dozen other people had turned to face them, tuning in to the conversation. "We're lucky here," she said. "At least our founders made that kind of thing impossible."

"You really believe that?" Olivier asked. His tone was polite, but he sounded incredulous.

Anna hesitated, wondering if the comparison would prove inflammatory—but she doubted that anyone here would think of the system that had ruined their lives as some kind of pinnacle of civilisation. "The wealth we get from Ceres isn't treated as an inheritance," she said. "The founders expected a return from their investment, and they got it—but they also accepted that Ceres itself wasn't conjured out of the vacuum by their money. If this rock belongs to anyone, it's not the children of whoever got in first with their robots; it's whoever chooses to live here and make the society work."

"And what if some group is perceived as not doing that?" Olivier replied. "Making trouble, rather than making things work?"

Anna inclined her head, conceding the point. "All right, that could happen. But at least it would depend on their own behaviour, not someone else's a century ago. I suppose what we've inherited is a strong utilitarian streak: if we had a choice between civil war and letting some perceived infraction pass unpunished, I think most of us would choose the latter."

Laurent smiled. "But that cuts both ways, doesn't it? If the Vestan majority were good utilitarians, they would have 'forgiven' our 'debt'...but if *we* were good utilitarians, we would have swallowed our pride and paid the tax. In the grand scheme of things, a tenth of the population becoming second-class citizens with a little less income hardly compares to the suffering caused by the war."

Before Anna could frame a diplomatic response to that, one of the onlookers, Céline, interjected disdainfully, "Utilitarianism is for theoreticians, not human beings."

"Really?" Anna lost interest in diplomacy and gave in to her combative streak. "Then how should human beings choose, say...a public health policy? If minimising harm across the whole society is so naïve and utopian, would you settle for whatever gives the best outcome for a few people closest to the decision-making process? Or would you prefer whatever we could achieve for ourselves in some kind of free-for-all scrabble to monopolise resources?"

Céline said, "Of course, we all accept something more equitable. But it's not because we put some health statistician's measures first. For the majority, it's a matter of enlightened self-interest to have a policy that doesn't play favourites."

Anna couldn't dispute that, but it was hardly the whole story. "And no one feels empathy beyond their immediate circle? No one thinks about what's just?"

"Do you have children?" Céline asked.

"I have a son."

"Can you honestly tell me that you view his welfare no differently from anyone else's?"

"Of course not!" Anna was bemused. "But I never expected Cererian society as a whole to give him special treatment. It's possible to love your own children more than anyone else's, and still cede power to a system that treats every child as interchangeable."

Céline said, "Only if you've never really felt the difference."

Anna was tempted to reply that if the system on Ceres had spared her from *feeling the difference*, that was probably one more point in its favour. But she had no way of knowing what raw wounds lay behind the woman's zeal.

Olivier said, "Enough politics. It's time to eat."

◐

When Anna arrived home, Chloe was staring at an overlay. It wasn't private, but Anna had no need to view it herself; she knew exactly what it would contain.

"On this scale, they barely seem to move from month to month," Chloe mused, holding up a thumb to gauge the corresponding interval on the trajectory.

"Or decade to decade," Anna replied.

"He should have just frozen himself, right here at home, and waited until interstellar travel became practical. We're sure to crack uploading in another hundred years."

Anna said, "That would have seemed so much lazier, though: lying around expecting other people to do all the work."

Chloe laughed curtly. "As opposed to lying around on a three-thousand-year cruise? Where the only thing that will keep you from being overtaken in a century or two is the collapse of civilisation?"

"If Vesta's any guide he might have made the right bet."

Chloe shut off the overlay and turned to face her. "So how was the party?"

"Interesting."

"Vesta is not your problem," Chloe said bluntly. "You shouldn't get involved."

"I'm not *involved*. Or do you think I'm going to fly off on a secret mission to try to overthrow the Vestan oppressors?"

"No one in this family would fly off on a fantasy mission, would they?"

Anna said, "The Vestans are part of our community now. What do you want—everyone keeping to themselves in their own little ghettoes?"

Chloe groaned. "They're hardly being persecuted here. They don't need your help."

"Who said anything about help?" Anna protested. "I just want to talk to someone with different experiences, now and then. I don't know why you're so...against that." She'd almost said *jealous*, but then it had felt like an unnecessary provocation.

"So Vesta's gone to hell, but that's no reason to be circumspect?"

Anna said, "It's reason to try to understand what's happening there."

"I don't want to understand," Chloe replied.

"You don't want to *understand?*"

Chloe was unrepentant. "They're welcome here, I'd never turn them away. But I don't want to feel their pain, or walk in their shoes, or see through their eyes."

Anna was bemused. "Because…?"

"Because that's the first step towards following them down: seeing the world the way they do."

"You think war is an infection, and we can catch it just by talking to them?"

Chloe said, "I know you think I'm some kind of bigot, but it's the opposite: I think Vestans are exactly like us. They had a life every bit as good as ours—just as safe, just as prosperous—and like us, a lot of bored, aimless people who'd never really found any purpose. But then they realised that they could fill that hole by inventing a grievance, and taking sides, and refusing to be swayed no matter what. Maybe you think we're immune to that kind of thing, but I don't."

"I don't think we're immune," Anna said, glad now that Chloe hadn't joined her at the party. "I just don't think the problem is contagious. And you're the one who's just offered a diagnosis. If forewarned is forearmed, how can more information about Vesta be a bad thing?"

"You're not after information. You're not going to be writing any thesis on the Vestan war."

"Really. So what am I after? You tell me."

Chloe was silent for a while, as if weighing up the cost of an honest response. "I think you're looking for a new family," she said. "Sasha's gone, and you're bored with me. So you want to find a new way to belong."

7

"**WE** should target the water supply," Laurent suggested. "Nothing too strong—just a mild enterotoxin."

"'Mild'?" Mireille made the word sound contemptible. "Why bother? No one would even notice."

"I think they'd notice a day or two of vomiting and diarrhoea," Laurent replied. "I meant 'mild' as opposed to wild-type cholera."

Camille was appalled. "What about children? What about ill people? Even if you don't kill someone by mistake, the risk is unacceptable."

"They need to know exactly what we're capable of," Mireille said coldly. "They need to know that no one's going to be able to relax and get on with their lives."

"But what are we trying to say?" Camille demanded. "Next time, we'll increase the potency and do real harm?" She had no intention of meekly accepting the vote, but she hadn't lost all sense of proportion. "If I believed that someone was threatening mass murder, I'd vote to lock them all up myself. We might as well march straight into prison."

Olivier said, "We need to show that we can make life uncomfortable, that's all. We want to be an irritant that pricks people's conscience—not an existential threat that will make them want to wipe us out."

Camille agreed with this assessment, but it was difficult to think of even a minor act of sabotage that couldn't be extrapolated into a horror show. Every Vestan had been instilled from an early age with an appropriate fear of their unmitigated environment—and anyone who messed with the integrity of the systems that kept the cold and the vacuum at bay could expect no mercy.

Laurent stretched his arms, then jumped up lightly to press his palms against the ceiling. They'd been sitting in Olivier's apartment for nearly three hours, doing nothing but talking, but Camille felt more weary than she did after ten hours at work. She'd hoped that the gathering would jolt them all out of their post-ballot malaise, but so far it had only intensified her sense of helplessness.

Laurent said, "What if we just turned the water bright red? We could use some harmless food dye that's been tested to the nth degree, so there's no risk of an adverse reaction."

Mireille groaned, but Camille laughed appreciatively. "I like it! On one level, it's just a light-hearted prank, so anyone who over-reacts will look foolish. But for the time it takes to pass through the system, no one will be thinking about anything else. You want to drink our blood? Go ahead: this is what it looks like."

"The message sounds right," Olivier concurred. "But what about the logistics? How do we get our hands on that much dye? And how can we get it into the water without it being filtered out— or triggering a purge of a few million litres because it looks like the purifiers failed?"

"How do they assess the water?" Laurent wondered. "Do they just test for things they're expecting?"

Camille was already looking it up. "They run specific assays for a few hundred compounds that can be present in Cererian ice, but they also do chromatography and mass spectrometry. If a new peak shows up, that's going to set alarm bells ringing...but we might still be able to steer a path through the blind spots." There was no such thing in analytic chemistry as a machine that told you every last constituent of a sample, without making a single assumption about the contents.

Mireille said, "You're talking about turning the water *red*. Do you really think noticing that is going to come down to mass spectrometry?"

"Hmm." Camille was fairly sure that there'd be no human eyes on the water; who'd pay to do a job like that? But a simple optical check of turbidity would still go off the scale in the presence of a visible dye.

"Is there some way we could delay the colour change?" Olivier asked. "Maybe use a precursor that only gets turned into a dye further downstream?"

"Turned into it by what?" Mireille pressed him.

"I don't know. Some kind of slow-acting catalyst?"

"This is starting to sound unfeasible," Camille conceded. "Large amounts of *anything*, bright red or otherwise, are going to be hard to make, hard to deliver, and hard to get past all the tests." Laurent's first idea had been more practical in one respect: a toxin relied on biological activity rather than any bulk physical property, using the body's sensitivity to amplify its effect.

Mireille said, "We should knock a few ice blocks out of orbit."

Laurent laughed. "You have a few spare rockets lying around, do you?"

"No," Mireille replied, "but it wouldn't be that hard to hack the attitude control jets. If you can turn a block far enough out of alignment, the next collision will throw it off-course. Sivadiers designed every component that makes the trading loop work, so let's see how people like living without it."

"We'd get by on recycling, wouldn't we?" Olivier brought up an overlay. "Oh. Not for long. Still…"

Camille was alarmed that he was even considering it. "I think a drought would be going too far," she said firmly.

Mireille lost patience. "All right, Goldilocks, what's your perfect solution?"

Camille reached desperately for a snappy reply. "Biological, like Laurent suggested…but smarter, safer, more precise. Biological, but benign."

Mireille scowled. "What does that even mean?"

For several long seconds, Camille could think of nothing more to say.

And then she had it.

ᘓ

"Let me check your suit." Gustave motioned to Camille to approach him.

She made her way warily across the workshop floor. The boots read her gait and timed their changes of adhesion almost as well as her own shoes, but her extra mass and bulk still made the process feel less secure than usual. "You don't think it's smart enough to check itself?" The suit was almost forty years old. They'd bought it on the grey market, and painted it jet black.

"It is unless it isn't, in which case it might not notice that it isn't." Gustave was old enough to have had first-hand experience with the model. "Stretch out your arms."

Camille did as he'd asked, and he bent over and placed an ear beside the right elbow joint. She wasn't sure whether to be amused or alarmed. "That's why I'm at more than ambient pressure? So you can listen for leaks?"

"Sssh." He finished the checks and straightened up.

"What happens if I get a puncture out there?"

"If it's from something small and slow, the fabric will repair itself."

"And if it's not small and slow?"

"The frictional heat will start a flash-fire. In a fraction of a second you'll be charcoal." Gustave smiled. "Much nicer than a slow asphyxiation."

"Absolutely."

Camille had walked on the surface just four times before, as a child. The first excursion had been thrilling, and the next two exciting enough, but on the fourth occasion, all the preparations and safety checks hadn't seemed worth it for a view she could get more clearly from an overlay. She'd never been afraid, though: she'd taken it for granted that her mother and her teachers wouldn't expose her to any real danger. Gustave was probably more qualified to keep her safe than any of the tour guides to whom she'd entrusted her life before. But the mere fact that she was acting clandestinely made her anxious out of all proportion to any reasonable assessment of the risk.

That, and the fact that for the first time in her life she'd be leaving the surface behind.

Gustave helped her strap on the gas jets. Their weight, on top of the suit, was enough to make her calves and lower back ache at the unaccustomed loading. "I've put the orbit of the ice block in by hand," he said. "It will be wiped from memory as soon as you're done. If you're caught, just say you were joyriding over the mines. The port's systems won't be able to contradict you; without a beacon, you won't be fast or shiny enough to register."

"Right." Camille's initial fantasy had involved obtaining a robot to do the job, but on reflection it wasn't entirely surprising that it was impossible to find a second-hand model with all its logs and safeguards disabled—ready to do its owner's bidding without a trace of accountability, whether that meant helping out with odd jobs around the home or bludgeoning random strangers to death.

Her comms found the jets' interface. She brought up the overlay and Gustave talked her through all the options. He could have flown this mission himself with his eyes closed, but the safety beacon implanted in his viscera, a prerequisite for his job at the port, rendered him incapable of stealth.

"Any questions?" he asked.

Camille shook her head. He led her to the airlock.

Every cycle of every airlock was logged, but Gustave had brought a cargo-handling robot into the workshop for an inspection a few days before, and now the fifteen-metre behemoth was ready to return to the surface. It would not power up until it had been delivered back into its working environment; so long as Camille got away quickly it would have nothing on her to tattle about. She clambered onto the machine and hunkered down behind the huge folded grippers; they looked like King Kong's monkey wrench. There were cameras in the airlock, but Gustave had assured her that this nook would be hidden by the bulk of the robot above her.

He called out to her, "Good luck."

The conveyor belt started up, carrying the robot forward. The ride itself was as smooth as any walkway's, and though the chassis creaked and shuddered a little, when the load was passed from the workshop's belt to the lock's Camille could barely detect the transition. The door slid into place behind her, then the suit's interface showed the ambient pressure dropping and the aural world shrank to the sound of her own breathing.

She felt the huge hydraulic lift begin its ascent, but once it was in motion it became imperceptible, and she wasn't even sure she had arrived until the outer door had risen high enough to admit a sudden blast of sunlight. Camille forced herself to stay flattened against the robot's hull, like a timid cockroach. She waited until the conveyor belt had deposited her insensate host on the rock, and then she crawled backwards and dropped to the surface. She gave the door a few seconds to come low enough to hide her from the cameras within, then she turned and marched briskly over the grey basalt, concentrating on the terrain, refusing to look up.

"All right," she muttered. She patted her tool belt to reassure herself that she hadn't dropped the payload somewhere and rendered the whole exercise pointless, then she invoked the jets' navigator and told it to execute Gustave's flight plan. Debris swirled around her for a second or two, the fractured facets of obsidian shards catching the sunlight, and then she was ascending.

The straps under her arms bore most of her weight, pressing into her flesh, while her legs dangled disconcertingly; it was like being lifted by a clumsy giant who couldn't manage a clean grip around her waist. Before she could begin to take in the aerial view of the site around the airlock, the horizon dropped away below the edge of her faceplate, leaving her with nothing to see but stars.

Camille focused on the navigator's overlay. The ice block Gustave had chosen for her had already suffered its last collision, leaving it in a high, slow orbit ready to be plucked by a cargo robot when needed. The schematic in front of her already showed her anticipated trajectory closing on the orbit, but it would take almost thirty minutes for her to match the block's altitude and speed.

The adrenaline rush of her illicit egress subsided, giving way to sober anxiety. But all she could do now was trust Gustave's claim that she was drab and sluggish enough not to elicit any interest from the port's specialised surveillance, which was more concerned with the prospect of misaligned cargo from a braking impact gone wrong than with the joyriders that everyone tutted about but made no real effort to stop.

She approached her target from the "night" side, its own shadow rendering it invisible against the blackness until she was so close that the starlit sheath appeared as a pale grey hexagon, looming larger at a disconcerting pace until she began to decelerate. The navigator eased her into a matching orbit but left a prudent gap of ten metres or so before surrendering control.

Camille had the jets administer a gentle puff that sent her inching her way towards the closest edge of the cube. The corners of the sheath were truncated into triangles where the attitude jets sat, safe from the impacts that struck the block head-on. The tiny tracking scopes fitted beside each jet only cared about a handful of guide stars; all she had to do was avoid blocking any of their lines of sight.

She was moving so slowly that she managed to get a gecko-grip with outstretched hands before her torso made contact. The sheath brought her to a halt but then rebounded, and when that failed to dislodge her she was dragged forwards, with the whole cycle repeating until she invoked the jets' software to administer some smart damping. Once she was still she clung to the spot, psyching herself into accepting that there'd be no danger in letting go with one hand, then she shut off the adhesion in her right glove and reached into her tool belt.

The spray gun couldn't pierce the sheath—but every sheath was guaranteed to be peppered with tiny holes from micrometeorites. Camille played the jet of lukewarm steam back and forth across the surface; frost clouds billowed away from the site, stretching far enough to leave the block's shadow and paint a fragment of a rainbow, pallid but surreal against the stars.

The concentration of the contaminant would be tiny, however much got through to the ice, but she'd designed it with care not to adhere to any of the adsorption purifiers or samplers it would be confronting further downstream. The only thing to which it would readily adhere was a particular kind of villus cell in the lining of the human intestine.

When the gun was empty, Camille checked the time. It would take her another forty minutes to return to the surface, but she had more than an hour's wait anyway, until Gustave's schedule allowed him to bring another robot through the lock.

☾

"Do you see it?" Camille asked impatiently. "Here!" She touched the spot.

Olivier remained silent. Perhaps his eyes were taking longer than hers to adapt to the dark.

"Oh, you're right." He laughed nervously, and slid his thumb back and forth over his inner arm, as if the fluorescent calligraphy might rub off.

"The J is a bit crooked," he complained.

"No, you're just tensing your muscles strangely," Camille retorted. "The morphogens are better at measuring the normal distance from cell to cell than you are."

"So when does yours show up?"

"Who knows? Not everyone will get enough of a dose."

Olivier said, "I think I should perform a thorough examination."

Camille undressed in the dark and lay down on the bed beside him. She thought the search would just be a game, but after a few seconds Olivier cried out in triumph and led her over to the mirror. The letters were on her lower back, angled obliquely. Choosing the site and the orientation had proved too hard; in the end, they'd settled for control over content rather than placement.

"*J'accuse*," she read, convincing herself that the upside-down mirror writing really was a faithful reproduction. "This is better than stamping it on everyone's forehead," she decided. "It's the element of surprise that's half the fun."

"Fun?" Olivier hesitated. "I hope that's how it's taken."

"More fun than six hours of cholera, or six weeks of drought."

"I'm not criticising the plan," he said. "But most recipients' first thoughts might not be 'Hooray! I don't have cholera!'"

Camille snorted. "Well, fuck them if they can't take a joke. I didn't think it was all that hilarious when I got mobbed in the emergency room."

"I know."

The doorbell rang. Olivier glanced at an overlay from the entrance camera. "Laurent?" he muttered.

"Ignore him," Camille suggested. "We don't all need to compare tattoos."

Laurent started pounding on the door. Olivier went to open it while Camille made herself presentable.

She heard the two men talking, too softly for her to make out the words, but the cadences were far from jovial or celebratory, and when she joined them in the sitting room the mood was sombre. "What is it?" she demanded.

Laurent said, "Mireille is dead."

"*What?*"

Olivier was hunched over on the couch, unable to speak, unable to look up at her.

"How? What happened?"

"She was in a nightclub," Laurent replied. "Mouthing off about the tax, and taunting some people..." He trailed off, but Camille understood: people for whom the message was suddenly visible, glowing on some patch of exposed skin.

Laurent continued. "Her friend said she was shouting, 'think about what's next!'"

Camille was light-headed. "But what did they do to her?" Throw a drink in her face? Throw a punch or two?

"They dragged her out and started beating her. By the time the robots pulled them off, she had a skull fracture and a blood clot. She died in the hospital, about an hour ago."

8

"TEN in a week." Pyotr whistled appreciatively. "That's a record."

Anna watched as Anton, the new trainee, dragged the pod out of the airlock. She said, "If the workload's getting too much, I can recommend putting a third team on standby."

"You should do that," Pyotr agreed. "Absolutely." He smiled and lowered his voice. "Some recognition of the higher demand might even bring my fees down."

"That's how it's meant to work," Anna replied, offended by the suggestion that she'd be doing him a favour. Then again, he was probably just needling her.

There was a faint banging from inside the pod. Pyotr sighed. "This is why I hate wrigglers. *Se calmer! Se calmer!*"

Anna left him to it and headed back to her office. She was halfway there, gliding along the middle of the corridor, when her Assistant spoke.

"There's some news I think you'll want to see."

It rarely interrupted her unbidden while she was travelling. Anna grabbed a guide rope and brought herself to a halt. "Show me," she replied.

A local news feed was carrying a report from a supposedly neutral source on Vesta. A ferry named the *Arcas* had visited the asteroid two weeks before on a scheduled trip, and the time it had spent docked there had passed without incident—but now the Vestan authorities were claiming that hundreds of "war criminals" were on board, and they were demanding that the *Arcas* return and surrender these people for prosecution.

Anna hung from the rope, unsure what to make of the story. The Vestans scrutinised everyone who came and went from these vessels—and their identification procedures weren't easily fooled, or there'd be no need for anyone to ride the stone river. Even anxious Sivadiers with the clearest of consciences who merely wished to be rid of the place only left by ferry in tiny numbers; Anna's Vestan friends had told her that most would be too afraid of being dragged out of the queue and accused of something they hadn't done.

When her shift was over, she called in on Olivier to hear his take on the incident. "The people they're after didn't board directly on Vesta," he explained, handing her a coffee. "The *Arcas* picked them up from deep space."

"You mean it plucked them off cargo stones!" Anna was prepared to be impressed by this audacious feat, but Olivier quashed the notion.

"No, that's not practical. These people weren't riders, they were waiting for a pre-arranged rendezvous."

He seemed sure of the facts. "So none of this took you by surprise?" she asked.

"I wasn't aware of the plan beforehand," Olivier replied. "I'm not some strategist-in-exile for the Vestan resistance! I just know people who've talked to people on the *Arcas* in the last few days."

"Right. So...who are these people on the *Arcas* that Vestan security are so keen to get back?" Anna caught herself. "Is that something you can tell me?"

"It's no secret now. The main one they're after is a man called Tavernier. *He's* the strategist. His identity became known about a year ago, and he must have been in hiding ever since."

"Why didn't he just become a rider?"

Olivier shrugged. "Maybe it was decided that his time was too valuable, or he was too important to face that risk."

Anna said, "I'm surprised that the owners of the ferry agreed to this." At the very least, it was going to be tense when the *Arcas* dropped in on the way back.

"The owners live on Mars, but they're sympathetic to the resistance," Olivier explained. "I suppose they decided it was worth the gamble. Vesta really can't afford to boycott the company; that would screw them almost as thoroughly as picking a fight with Ceres."

"I've sometimes wondered if we should use the ice trade for leverage," Anna admitted. "We could cope without new building material—"

Olivier cut her off. "That would be crazy. Apart from the delay in any impact downstream, I can promise you that innocent people would go thirsty long before anyone in power."

"OK." Anna set down the empty coffee mug and rubbed her eyes. "Well, the *Arcas* clearly won't be turning around before it comes here. So if they're serious about wanting this Tavernier, they'll have to send an extradition request."

Olivier was amused. "I think they've got the message on that front. The courts have turned down, what, fifty so far?"

"Every case is decided on its merits," Anna insisted. "If they have real evidence that he's a war criminal, it's not impossible that he'll be returned."

"I doubt that's how Vestan security will be looking at it."

Anna said, "Maybe. But what else can they do?"

Olivier hesitated, as if unsure whether she meant the question seriously. Eventually he realised that she did.

"Come after him," he said. "Give chase."

9

"**TEN** years isn't nothing," Laurent said warily. "That's the longest sentence they could give."

"For *manslaughter!*" Céline's face was distorted with contempt. "I should slit a few Taxer throats and see if I get manslaughter!"

Angelique, Mireille's sister, put an arm around her mother, but Céline threw it off. Camille was starting to wish that they'd chosen to meet in someone's apartment instead; this café was close enough to the courthouse that the family had been able to stagger in while they were still numb with shock—but it was far too public for what was unfolding as the shock wore off.

A man who'd been stealing glances from a nearby table approached Céline. "I'm so sorry about your daughter," he said. "I've never felt so angry and ashamed as when I heard that news."

Céline stared through him.

"I've decided to join Fair Share," he added. "I was thinking about it for a while, and now—"

"Fuck off!" Céline screamed. "If you want to give me charity, just bring me a knife!"

The man recoiled and hurried out of the café. The other customers averted their gaze.

Olivier whispered, "I'm so glad now that I didn't join." Camille reached down and punched him on the leg. Members of FS agreed to share their total tax liability equally among themselves, irrespective of ancestry. The last Camille had heard, almost five percent of Vesta's untaxed population had signed up—as a gesture of solidarity, and a defiant nose-thumb to the New Dispensation Movement—but only about a tenth of the Sivadiers, and there was a lot of pressure on them to drop out. She thought it was grossly unfair to dismiss the whole idea as condescending, but coming right after the murder, the timing had made the concept doubly offensive to those who were inclined to take offence.

Céline began weeping in long, angry sobs. Camille couldn't think of anything she could say that would have the slightest chance of diminishing the woman's pain.

If she hadn't deployed the graffiti virus, Mireille might still be alive. But what were the Sivadiers meant to do? Meekly accept the status quo in silence, with FS rubbing salt in the wound by neutralising any claim of actual disadvantage? Ten percent, five percent, one percent…it made no difference. Either the distinction was erased and they became Vestans like any other Vestans again—or they remained Freeloaders, parasites and vermin. Fair game.

After forty minutes, Olivier could take no more. He leant towards Céline and spoke softly. "I'm so sorry, but we have a shift at the hospital," he said, including Camille in his lie.

Céline nodded blankly, but Angelique rose to kiss them on their cheeks. As they hurried away, Olivier said quietly, "We need to calm this down. No more escalation, however benign it seems."

Camille frowned. "And you're calling the shots now?"

"No, I'm expressing an opinion."

"So you think we should be intimidated into doing nothing?"

Olivier stopped dead, almost colliding with her on the rope. He said, "I've just spent an hour listening to talk about slitting people's throats. Our last effort got one of us murdered and a new security chief installed. Doesn't any of that tell you that we need to be thinking things through more carefully?"

"It's out of your hands," Camille said. "And mine. We planned one tiny action, but no one's put us in charge of the whole show."

"I never assumed we were in charge of anything. I'm just trying to have a rational discussion about the things I think we ought to be advocating." He sounded puzzled, and even a bit hurt.

"There's something I haven't told you," Camille admitted. "They wouldn't let me, because you're still being vetted. So you have to keep this between us."

Olivier stared back at her. "Vetted? *By whom?*"

She looked around; there was no one in earshot, for whatever that was worth. "There's a much larger group than ours; they've been organising since the referendum. They know we're behind the virus…and one of their recruiters approached me last week."

"So you're part of this group now? But you weren't meant to tell me?" Olivier emitted a curt laugh of disbelief that choked as it turned to anger.

Camille could think of no pleasant way to explain the situation. "Because you're not descended from any Sivadiers, they're a bit paranoid that you might be some sort of…"

"Spy?"

"Yes. I told them that was absurd, but they said I could hardly be objective."

Olivier replied icily, "So how, exactly, are they going to determine whether I'm truly against the Sivadier Tax, or whether I cleverly started screwing a Sivadier two years before there was any such thing, just so I could infiltrate their then-nonexistent movement and sabotage it from within?"

Camille shook her head. "I have no idea."

Olivier said, "Maybe I'm the one who should be vetting them. Even if they're not spies themselves, I might not actually want to get involved with their grand plans."

"I shouldn't have said anything," Camille declared forlornly. "They have their procedures, and they have to be satisfied with everyone. For all I know, they might have spent twice as long investigating me."

Olivier's expression softened. "Yeah. Maybe my ego's just a little bruised." He glanced back down the corridor. "We should keep moving, or we're going to bump into someone we know and get caught out as lying deserters. And who knows what our new commander-in-chief would do to people like that?"

10

"**YOU** heard about the warship leaving Vesta?" Chloe asked as Anna came through the door.

"Yes." Anna had been told the news at least a dozen times already—and she'd given up trying to persuade people to stop using the word "warship". The *Scylla* had started life as a ferry on the Mars-Vesta-Ceres run, but it had been out of service for a decade. That it had actually been repaired and refurbished was a surprise even to the people who paid attention to such things, and no one really knew what its current capabilities were. "But there's no reason to assume that it can catch up with the *Arcas*, or get close enough to do any damage."

"Maybe not," Chloe conceded. "But if it can't catch them in mid-flight, that could mean the *Scylla* asking to dock here."

Anna had been thinking of nothing else all day. "Anyone's free to enter, so long as we can be confident that they're not bringing in weapons." That was the official policy; all the leeway, of course, was in the word *confident*. "If they want to make their case in court, if they're carrying some warrant with Tavernier's name on it…"

Chloe laughed. "What about a virus with Tavernier's name on it?"

"You think they'd be that brazen?" Anna flopped onto the couch and felt the oobleck beneath the skin yield then stiffen. "They'd just come here and murder him?"

"If they could get away with it, why not?"

"Vestan security agents running around Ceres wouldn't have much chance of keeping a low profile. If they were so keen to assassinate him, they'd be better off paying someone who was already here."

"True." Chloe brought up an overlay from an astronautics specialist who'd been tracking the two ships. "So maybe they really are counting on an interception. It's not impossible." There were still big error bars on all the projections.

Anna felt sick. "You do know there's no prospect of them boarding the *Arcas* by force?" That wasn't just her own, amateur assessment; the same specialist had spelled out the kinds of spoiling manoeuvres that would render it impossible even for a robot to gain entry. "If there's any kind of 'interception', it will mean destroying the whole ship."

Chloe pondered this. "Unless the people they're after choose to give themselves up. If I had a choice between being arrested and being slaughtered along with eight hundred other passengers, I think I'd try to minimise the bloodshed. Not to mention clutching at a slim chance of surviving, myself."

"Of course." Short of a clean escape, it was the best outcome Anna could envision. "But the question is whether they get a chance to see it that way. The *Scylla* would have to make the offer at a time when the people on the *Arcas* would accept that those really were the only two choices."

Chloe smiled grimly. "Which people on the *Arcas*, though? Vesta's most wanted, the crew who chose to take the risk of picking them up, or the other passengers—who probably didn't even know what they'd be in for? Because if it's up to the last group, they might just want to stop and hand over the war criminals sooner rather than later."

11

"**IF** we succeed in taking out both collectors, that will mean *thirty percent* power cuts." Nicolas paused, as if he was expecting a round of rousing cheers at this point, but his team of would-be saboteurs just stared back at him anxiously.

"But that success will only come from discipline," he continued. "*Nothing* is to be written down. *Nothing* is to be stored in any device. All navigation will be by eye and hand only. Whatever equipment is captured, there must be no data trail."

Camille lost patience; the man had been talking for fifteen minutes and he still hadn't addressed the most important issue. "The collectors aren't going to be sitting there undefended," she said.

"That's not your concern."

"Excuse me?"

Nicolas regarded her with a mixture of irritation and pity. "You need to focus on your own instructions, nothing else. Your part of the mission will be made crystal clear to you, but if you start speculating about other matters that's only going to distract you."

"Getting caught or killed might distract me too, don't you think?"

Olivier glanced at her, a look half supportive, half imploring her to tone it down.

Their cell commander rose from his seat and geckoed a few steps across the circle. "What you did with the ice was a nice little calling card. No one's forgotten your initiative there. But we don't have room in the movement for prima donnas with mixed consciousness. You need to concentrate on the job you've been given, and stop expecting to know the whole plan."

Camille felt her cheeks burning. *Mixed consciousness?* She'd have gladly paid triple the tax for the right to laugh in the face of every buffoon who spoke that way. But this was how it worked now. She avoided the gaze of her embarrassed comrades and stared evenly back at Code Name Nicolas.

"I understand," she said. "I know how to follow orders."

☾

Three days later, lying in bed in Olivier's apartment, they compared roles. Camille's task was to sever a data cable that she assumed was part of the new radar system; she wouldn't even need to go up to the surface. Olivier was being sent out to one of the dishes, carrying some kind of device that he'd yet to lay eyes on. It was hard to imagine how a bomb could do much damage to such a large structure, with no air to carry shock waves and the dish itself so insubstantial that any localised force would tear it in one spot rather than shatter it in its entirety. But after debating the question for a while—and resisting the urge to perform any incriminating online searches—Olivier guessed that his payload might be some kind of electromagnetic pulse generator. A strong enough induced current could melt the fine mesh that supported the collector's membrane, turning it into a gossamer rag that the solar wind alone could blow out of shape.

"It's not fair," Camille said. "You're the one who'll be taking all the risks."

"As you did, with the virus."

"It's different now."

Olivier laughed. "Come on, don't be greedy! Share the fun!"

Camille put a hand on his cheek. "If I'd been caught, I could have passed as a joyrider. No one was going to harm me. Those days are gone, my love."

Olivier was silent for a while. Then he said, "This will prove it, though."

"Prove what?"

"That I'm committed, whatever my ancestral deficiencies."

Camille scowled. "Fuck that! And fuck every last idiot on this rock who can't stop thinking about people's pedigree."

Olivier just smiled and ignored her outburst. "The target is fair," he mused. "No one's going to die from thirty percent power cuts. They'll just be mightily pissed off, and finally understand that they have to take this seriously." A month before he'd been talking about de-escalating; now he sounded as if he was trying to psych himself into his new role.

Camille said, "The real question is what *taking this seriously* entails: dropping the tax, or digging their heels in."

"Digging their heels in over one percent of general income?"

"It's not about the money," she said. "It's about how attached they've grown to Denison's story. Their families were cheated into carrying the Freeloaders, and for a century no one was punished for that crime. Now that justice is finally being done, how can they go back to the old order?"

"Who cares about justice if the game-world servers can't run?"

Camille prodded him, mock-reprovingly. "You're such a cynic!"

"And you're such a prima donna."

She punched him on the arm, hard enough to make him flinch. "My consciousness is more conscious than your consciousness."

"Ah, but how many conches could a consciousness conch if a consciousness could conch conches?"

Camille said, "I'll pay you a hundred dollars to shout that out at the next cell meeting, the first time Nicolas uses the C word."

Olivier considered the offer, and came back with a counterproposal. "A thousand dollars—and I only have to do it if he says the word three times."

"Coward."

"Miser."

Camille said, "All right: a thousand dollars. You're on."

12

"GUSTAVE is on the *Arcas!*" Olivier announced elatedly. "*Gustave!*" He took Anna by the shoulders and kissed her on both cheeks.

"Wonderful," she replied. She had no idea who he was talking about, but it seemed like a safe bet that this wasn't bad news. She followed Olivier into the apartment; half a dozen of his friends were gathered in the living room, and they all appeared equally delighted.

"Gustave Bodel is the reason most of us got away," Olivier explained. "He smuggled hundreds of people up to the surface and out onto the cargo blocks. Maybe thousands, if you count everyone still in transit."

"We've only just heard," Laurent added. "Vestan security didn't have him on the list of 'criminals' they were demanding to be returned, so the other passengers were keeping quiet about his presence."

"Right." Anna didn't know quite what to say. "I'm glad to hear that your friend is almost out of danger."

"Almost?" Stéphane was having none of this cautious language. "The only way the *Arcas* isn't going to make it is if the *Scylla* is packed with engineers who've been frantically designing a new super-weapon…which will be ready for deployment in the next three days."

Anna wasn't going to argue the point and dampen the spirits of the gathering. The *Arcas* had started to decelerate in preparation for its rendezvous with Ceres, but the *Scylla* was continuing to power ahead—and that strategy alone was rapidly narrowing the gap between the ships. The pursuers hadn't literally forfeited their chance to dock at Ceres themselves; they could always double back later, at great expense in time and energy. But it proved that they hadn't given up hope of drawing close enough for a destructive encounter.

"Gustave will make it," Monique insisted, as if the man's skills that brought so many of his comrades safely to Ceres could somehow work in his own favour now.

"There's one thing about the riders that always puzzled me," Anna confessed. "Once the authorities knew what was happening, why didn't they start monitoring the cargo more closely?"

Céline said, "Because they were never serious about stopping the riders. If Sivadiers wanted to leave, good riddance to them."

"But I thought they wanted to arrest the riders."

"If we'd shown up trying to board a ferry, they would have," Laurent explained. "And if they'd heard that anyone high up in the resistance was heading for a cargo block, they'd stake it out. But minor foot soldiers were allowed to slip away. That was the choice: exile by the slowest, most dangerous route, or risk whatever happened when they came for you."

Anna was about to observe that perhaps the sainted Gustave had never faced much risk himself if the authorities had wanted him to keep shepherding Sivadiers into exile, but she caught herself in time. Regardless of the demands of tact, humility alone should have silenced her. What risks would *she* have borne, if she'd found herself at Gustave's end of the stone river?

"So in three days," she said, "I think I can guess who's going to be the guest of honour at your welcoming party."

13

CAMILLE glided homewards from the clinic by her usual route, recognising none of the people she passed but wondering if any of them might be a little more attentive than she was. Perhaps she'd left a faint impression as someone who often came this way, at this time. The question, then, was whether that skein of casual observers was woven tightly enough to pin down her movements.

When the moment arrived, she had no way to be certain that the cameras around her were jammed; she'd been told that the interference would be device-specific, leaving personal links unimpaired. But it would encompass a wide enough area to avoid bringing security drones down upon her immediately; with dozens of kilometres of corridors disappearing from the surveillance system, the black-out zone would offer no immediate clue as to the site of actual mischief.

She waited until she was alone before she grabbed the guide rope and boosted her speed, propelling herself forward repeatedly. She passed the turnoff to her home, and continued on for another hundred metres or so until she reached the entrance to a maintenance tunnel. A sign in red letters warned that only authorised personnel should enter, but there were thousands of these tunnels across the whole warren—and not even the graffiti virus had been enough to prompt the engineering department to fit them all with biometrically secured hatches. All she had to do was slip between two chains, parting them wearing a pair of latex gloves that she'd pocketed at the clinic.

The tunnel was about three metres wide, with no guide rope down the centre, and no lighting at all. Maintenance robots, or the rare human worker, would bring their own illumination, but Camille switched to passive thermal vision as the light from the corridor behind her faded away. In infrared the scene was like an endoscopic scan, with opalescent walls revealing hints of the city's pulsing vasculature. She let herself descend until she could push herself up from the hand rails spaced evenly along the floor—cool silhouettes against the heat behind them—but the same kind of rails appeared on all eight surfaces of the tunnel's octagonal cross-section. With the architecture so symmetrical, her sense of the vertical wavered, and a part of her brain started labelling the axis of the tunnel as "up".

Forbidden to use her inertial navigation chip, she had nothing to guide her but the count of hatches she passed. None of them would open up on anything more strategic than a heating pipe; the cable that carried data from the radar system was far from the reach of prying hands in any unprotected space like this. But when she counted hatch seventy-three on her lower right, she grabbed a rail, brought herself to a halt, and yanked the flap open.

Camille surveyed the glowing pipes and dimmer crevices in the rock in front of her, bringing back Nicolas's verbal description of the correct cranny: "a triangular aperture to the upper left, well above ambient temperature." The natural rock in which these pipes had been laid did not enclose them all snugly, as if it had been poured around them like concrete; however precise the tunnelling robots had been, there were endless flaws and unplanned interstices in the space they had opened up, as pieces of rock had crumbled or fallen away rather than staying put to be diamond-carved into perfect geometrical forms.

Camille had no idea who had first mapped this maze of micro-caves and tunnels—or how the map had been acquired by her superiors—but it wasn't her role to fret over those details. She had exactly one purpose: to get her job right, so Olivier could do his own in safety. The mole she coughed up from its hiding place was less than a centimetre long. It would have no option but to use inertial guidance and stored coordinates, but it was fitted with a melt-on-tamper device that wouldn't have been too congenial inside her own skull. She fought back a fresh set of qualms: *Could the person who'd printed the thing be identified?* Though it hadn't been put together from factory components, its raw materials would still comprise a kind of signature. But that wasn't her problem.

She pinched the mole's midriff to wake it, and waited for it to squirm a little as proof of a successful boot. Then she slid it into the crevice. For a moment it remained where she'd lodged it, merely undulating slightly, then it vanished from sight.

Camille closed the hatch, turned around, and retreated as fast as she could. She was running ten seconds ahead of schedule—but that still only gave her three minutes before enough jammers were expected to be found and shut down to render her movements visible again. She needed to be home, out of the cameras' view, or the surveillance software would spot the continuity error in her journey, and pluck her out from the masses for special attention.

Near the entrance to the maintenance tunnel she paused in the dark, listening. The thrum of a guide rope being plucked echoed down the corridor. She waited interminable seconds for the body to glide past, then she advanced—only to retreat again. There were voices approaching, slowly. Painfully slowly.

Camille huddled in the shadows, watching the seconds flicker in the corner of her vision. She had barely two minutes to get home. Less than two. One and a half.

The dawdlers passed. She waited for them to move far enough beyond the tunnel for there to be some chance that they'd fail to make the connection when she overtook them out of nowhere. *One minute.* How fast would she need to dash, and how innocent could she make it seem? Could she leave no other impression to be summoned from memory—once the call went out for every citizen to report suspicious movements—than a blur of a woman rushing past, presumably in urgent need of a toilet?

When she entered the corridor, she knew it was too late. She took hold of the guide rope and accelerated gently, ensuring that the people ahead would feel her approach rather than her moment of attachment, but it was plain now that she couldn't make it home in the next fifty seconds without turning herself into an indelible spectacle.

As she closed on the dawdlers, one of them glanced back at her. The man's expression was neutral but not unfriendly. There were six people in the group, chatting pleasantly, taking their time. And they were almost at the turn-off to her apartment.

Camille slowed down a little, waiting for them to pass the junction, then she sped up and drew closer, listening for snatches of intelligible conversation rising out of the overlapping voices and insider shorthand. *Thirty seconds.* The jammers' active life could only be guessed; she might already be under scrutiny. Or she might have forty, fifty seconds more.

She caught up with the group.

"Excuse me?" *Twenty seconds.*

"Yes?" The woman's expression was open, welcoming: they weren't going to snub her and doom the whole plan. Camille imagined a scalpel slicing her own eyeball, to keep herself from bursting into tears of gratitude.

"I heard you mention *Crystal Pavilions*, and I just wanted to know what you thought."

"You don't read player reviews?" a man asked, his tone more bemused than suspicious.

"You know..." Camille shrugged ambiguously, not quite suggesting that they could ever be rigged. "I was going to try it out for a day, but there's so many times I've got hooked on something, and ended up heavily invested in it, only to find out a month later that it's all just..." She made do with a gesture again. She didn't know the right jargon, and she'd make a fool of herself if she improvised.

The woman who'd greeted her rolled her eyes empathetically. "I've been there!"

Camille detached from her body and drove it like a puppet, putting it through all the right moves, only resorting to speech when there was no other way to lubricate the interaction. The group of friends, evangelising on their favourite topic, remained unhurriedly rooted to the spot. Given their varying pace as she'd witnessed it, they could easily have arrived at this junction much earlier during the blackout— early enough to bump into Camille on her way home from work, and for all of them to have lingered here for a few minutes of conversation. So long as she'd seemed engaged at the moment the cameras started up again, there was a chance she wouldn't raise any flags at all.

The *Pavilion* fans might have proselytised forever, but she was the one who'd look suspicious if she showed no sign of wanting to move on. Once she'd heard enough detail that she could plausibly claim that she'd been talked out of her reluctance to take a trial run, she thanked everyone warmly and excused herself.

The smile on her face lingered naturally as she headed home at a normal pace; she didn't need to devise a new mask for the cameras. When she closed her apartment door behind her, fragments of encomia were still running through her head. The next time she bumped into these people there would be no hope of faking it: she would absolutely have to try out the game.

But not yet. A sudden change in her comms usage pattern—at precisely the time when a saboteur might be desperate to know if the most power-hungry servers had gone down—could place her, at least, in some second tier of suspects worthy of ongoing extra attention.

She showered, then brought up an overlay with a news feed to watch while she ate. For the moment, everything interesting was happening elsewhere: the latest developments in various political disputes in different nations on Earth took more than half an hour to summarise. Camille sat and marvelled at the thought that she'd once judged it vital to stay on top of all this nonsense. Earth might as well have circled another star for all it mattered to her life.

By midnight there was still no mention of anything on Vesta more dramatic than an upset win in the volleyball leagues. She contemplated shutting off the feed and heading for Olivier's apartment; he'd told her he expected the whole thing to be over in a couple of hours, and though a visit now would be a departure from their routine, that would hardly be enough to rise up out of the background noise to condemn her.

Then the feed's narrator said, "A male suspect has been taken into custody, attempting to re-enter the city from the surface after mounting an attack on vital infrastructure. The engineering department has confirmed that a solar collector went offline almost fifty minutes earlier, but they were able to draw on stored power to keep supplies level for that period—preventing the act of sabotage from becoming widely known, in order to safeguard an operational response that was still in progress. The suspect will face an initial hearing within the next eight hours, and multiple charges are expected to be laid in coming days."

That was it. No name, no face, no eye-witness shots of the arrest or subsequent movements of the prisoner. As the feed moved on to other matters, Camille stared into the flow of images, numb at first, then cursing softly. Her shoulders began to tremble, but she forced herself to be still. If it was Olivier, at least he was still alive. If it was the other saboteur, anything was possible.

She could not go to his apartment now: the timing would be too suspicious. The lack of detail in the news story could have been a deliberate attempt to flush out a response. Camille buried her face in her arms, trying to remain disciplined. If he was free and safe, he would contact her as soon as he was able. If he was in custody, his name would have to be disclosed at the first hearing. Either way, she had no choice but to be patient.

She lay on the couch, letting the feed play on in case some new detail was announced. *This was it*, she decided. They'd taken their stand, they'd made a grand gesture, but it wasn't worth the risks to push it any further. Mireille was dead, and someone was in prison. Whoever it was, the cost was already too high. Let the Taxers wallow in their triumph for another decade, or another generation, until they stumbled on another, more satisfying form of self-aggrandisement.

There was a knock on the door, soft and tentative. Camille felt blood drain from her face before she even knew why; she was thinking of Laurent's visit, bearing bad news. She couldn't bring herself to look through the security camera; she just propelled herself across the room and swung the door open.

Olivier said, "I know it's late, but I needed to be with you."

Camille waited until he'd closed the door behind him before she started weeping.

"What?" he teased her. "What's this about? Don't worry about the other guy, we'll find him a good lawyer."

"What happened out there?"

"To him? I don't know. It all went smoothly for me. And we might not have shut down the game servers, but someone's going to get an image of that melted dish online eventually, and it's going to hit hard."

"We have to…" Camille faltered.

"Keep up the pressure on the bastards? Absolutely!" Olivier geckoed his feet and lifted her up into his arms, elated. "Nothing on Vesta is safe now. That's what they need to understand. Everything is in our hands!"

14

"*ARCAS*, you are cleared to dock at bay seventeen. Can you confirm receipt of the approach route?"

"Confirmed. Thank you Ceres. See you in two hours."

The image of Captain Burton's face blinked out. Anna felt her jaw aching and wondered if she'd been beaming idiotically throughout the exchange. Her Assistant could have handled the whole procedure, but she was damned if she was going to spend this moment in history napping in her hammock while the machines swapped data.

Her Assistant said, "Incoming call from the *Scylla*."

"Ha!" Anna slapped her knee in delight. "It's a bit early to be reserving a dock, at their velocity."

"Will you take the call or should I?"

She composed herself. "I'll take it."

A middle-aged man's face appeared, tagged as "Captain Vieira." He hesitated, perhaps unsettled by the lack of synchrony in their eye contact; his ship was still so far behind the *Arcas* that the time lag was perceptibly longer.

"Go ahead *Scylla*," Anna encouraged him. "It's disconcerting, but we'll do our best."

"Ceres, I have a request to make. Over."

Anna almost smiled; she'd never had a conversation before where this convention was necessary.

"*Scylla*, please state your request. Over."

"The *Arcas* is en route to dock at your facility. We have presented documentation to Ceres law enforcement establishing that more than two hundred war criminals are on board. Accordingly, we ask that you refuse the *Arcas* permission to dock. Over."

Anna resisted the temptation to lapse into sarcasm. "Ceres law enforcement has advised the port authority that these matters can only be pursued through the courts. I have no instructions to turn the *Arcas* away. Over."

"Ceres, I request that you reconsider. Over."

Anna frowned, momentarily lost for words.

"*Scylla*, your request is denied. The *Arcas* has permission to dock. This is not negotiable. Over."

Vieira's face showed no surprise at her reply, but then why was he going through the motions? Just to make some superior fractionally less angry that he'd failed to catch his quarry?

"Ceres, I wish to inform you that we've made some adjustments to our outgoing cargo stream. Over."

Anna wondered if she'd misheard him somehow, but the audio was coming through flawlessly. What kind of *non sequitur* was this—unless he was threatening to pelt her with blocks of stone, in some weirdly ineffectual fit of pique?

"*Scylla*, can you clarify the nature of these adjustments? Over."

"We've moved new faces to the axes of rotation. All other parameters are unaltered. Over."

Vieira's demeanour remained deadpan. Anna invoked a filter to hide her own reaction, even before she fully understood the significance of his words.

Riders rode the stone blocks glued to the axes of rotation. While each of the other four faces of the sheathed cubes suffered collisions, the "north and south poles" were safe throughout the trip.

"*Scylla*, what is the purpose of this adjustment? Over."

Vieira said, "Evening-out wear on the cargo sheaths. Over."

The sheaths were systematically rotated when they were reused at the end of each run. As a pretext, this wasn't even half believable.

"*Scylla*, could you please supply logs of these changes. Over." Whatever the Vestans had done, there ought to be enough propellant left in the attitude jets to reverse it.

"Ceres, we would be happy to comply with your request if you comply with ours. Over."

Anna's bowels turned to ice. The conversation had never been heading anywhere else, but part of her had been clinging to the hope that somehow it would veer away—that the sheer formality of their words would render it impossible to utter a threat of mass murder.

"*Scylla*, we will contact you again shortly. Over and out." She cut the link and shouted at her Assistant, "Get me the Cargo Engineer!"

Mira listened patiently as Anna stumbled over her words. "Can they really do that?" Anna asked. "Without our knowledge, without our permission?"

"All the security is against tampering by third parties," Mira replied. "And outgoing cargo is the exporter's responsibility, until it enters the controlled space of the recipient."

"But if they've sent commands to the attitude jets…there must be logs in the jets that we can read?"

"Not if they've wiped them, or corrupted them. Give me a second." Mira looked away, interacting with another overlay. "I've just queried the closest few blocks; the others will take time to reach. The ones I can see have empty logs."

Anna's spirits rose. "Could that mean this whole thing's a bluff? There was no flipping?"

"The logs shouldn't be empty—they should have a record of the adjustments that centred the faces for all the collisions over the trip. The only certain thing is that they've been wiped."

"Fuck." Anna had left her hammock to stand geckoed to the floor, but now she felt as if she was in free fall.

Mira said, "Wait, I can check propellant levels."

"They can't fake that?"

"Not unless they planned all of this three years ago, when they filled the jets at the start of the trip. I can query the levels directly from the hardware, and we know how much should have been used for legitimate trimming."

Anna waited. *It was a bluff, it had to be a bluff.* If they'd really been willing to go after the riders, they could have done it at any time. The fact that Olivier, Laurent and the others were safe on Ceres was proof that the Vestans didn't just slaughter their enemies when they were fleeing.

Mira turned back to face her. "There's unexplained propellant loss. Enough to do what they're claiming."

"Is that proof that they actually did it?" Anna pressed her.

Mira hesitated. "No. They could have vented the same amount doing pointless adjustments with no net effect."

Anna struggled to see a way forward. "Suppose they did flip the blocks. What's the fastest way we could identify the precise faces the riders are on?"

"The heat signature's invisible at this distance. We'd need to send some kind of probe to tour the cargo belt."

There were collisions every few days—each with a one-in-four chance now of killing a rider. A probe would take months.

"We could shift a pair of non-axial faces onto the axis, for every block," Mira suggested. "Chosen at random. If they really flipped them all, at least that would put half the riders back in safe positions."

Anna was horrified—and sorely tempted. Gambling with people's lives was abhorrent, but better Russian roulette than a bullet in every chamber. Except…they wouldn't know for sure if they were taking bullets out, or adding them. "What if they didn't do it? Or they only flipped some fraction?" The counter-move would save half the riders on flipped blocks, but it would have the opposite effect, with certainty, for those on every block that had been left unflipped.

"Then we're screwed," Mira conceded.

"There must be something else we could do with the jets," Anna begged her. "Nudge the blocks out of orbit, so they miss the collisions? Or just turn them edge-on?"

"There's nowhere near enough propellant for the first. And collisions where the impact isn't spread over a full face are known to shatter both the cargo and the helper rock. There might be a small chance of surviving that, if the pods remain intact and we can track them down—but again, if we do it to anyone who was actually safe on the axis to start with…"

Anna was silent; she was out of ideas. If the Vestans could wipe the logs remotely then they had probably also patched the controlling software to veto any commands to the jets that they didn't authorise themselves. A counter-hack might be possible, but to what end? Without knowing exactly which blocks had been flipped, there was no manoeuvre guaranteed not to make things worse.

Mira said, "How many riders do you think are in transit?"

The arrivals had reached one or two daily, but the conflict had worsened even further since those people had departed. "Three thousand, four thousand," Anna guessed. Her legs were beginning to cramp, but she stayed rooted to the spot.

"Can you...negotiate something?" Mira asked tentatively. "Maybe the *Arcas* will agree to hand over the people there are warrants for?"

"I'll talk to them."

Anna raised Captain Burton.

He said, "Tell them anything you need to. Tell them that when they dock, we'll all be waiting there on Ceres by the airlock, in manacles."

A promise like that would be meaningless. "What if you bypass Ceres, and coordinate a voluntary boarding by the *Scylla?*"

Burton shook his head. "They're not interested in sending a boarding party. If they ever get so close that we can't dodge their missiles, they'll just blow us apart."

"I know there's that risk," Anna conceded. "But there are thousands of riders—"

"I'm not the one endangering them!" Burton snapped back. "My responsibility is to my passengers and crew. If you're asking me to commit suicide and to take them all with me, I'm respectfully going to have to decline."

Anna said, "And what will you do if I withdraw your permission to dock?"

"Do it anyway. And I don't think you have time to block every bay."

"I don't need to block the bays. I could seal all the airlocks." Anna could feel blood pulsing in her neck. She was talking about slamming the door in the face of people who'd come to her seeking protection. Needing protection. "If you're unable to disembark, what do you think will happen when the *Scylla* flies past?"

"You'd hang us out to dry? You'd let them murder eight hundred people?"

"And you'd let them murder four thousand?"

Burton said, "You don't know that they're not bluffing about that."

"And you don't know that they'd refuse a boarding party," Anna countered. No one had to die. They just had to organise a peaceful rendezvous.

"We're coming in," Burton replied. "What you do with the airlocks is on your conscience."

The overlay cut out. Anna felt herself sag as if she'd been struck. This decision was beyond her—but who could she defer to? This was her job, no one else's.

She closed her eyes. That Olivier had made her feel as if she knew these people didn't help. How could she stand back and let the Vestans crush Camille between boulders? But how could she conspire with them to keep Gustave locked out of Ceres until they blew the *Arcas* apart?

The numbers were clear. Unless Vieira was bluffing. But the threat to the *Arcas* wasn't certain either. If all things were equal, she had to protect the riders. Unless Vieira planned to cheat her: to hold back the data about the flips. But why would he do that? Why would Vesta needlessly court opprobrium from across the inhabited worlds?

But wouldn't the same fear of sanctions keep them from butchering the riders, regardless—even if the *Arcas* was given shelter? Surely the whole thing had to be a bluff?

She didn't know that. She couldn't know that.

"Call the *Arcas*," she told her Assistant. The scheduled docking was less than ninety minutes away.

Burton appeared, stony faced.

"Can we fake this?" she asked. "Make it look as if you've been denied entry—but get everyone out in spacesuits? The *Arcas* goes into a holding orbit, the *Scylla* flies by and…does what it does…but no one is on board. We'll bring you all in, in secret, and hide you for as long as it takes to be sure that the riders are safe."

Burton hesitated. Anna struggled to decipher his expression. He did not seem affronted by the plan, by the dangers the evacuation would pose, but he was weighing up something.

"All right," he said. "We can do this."

Anna told her Assistant to inform the *Scylla* that the *Arcas* would not be docking, then she had it coordinate the evacuation with the ferry's navigator.

No one could leave the *Arcas* until the engines shut off and it was orbiting Ceres, but they could all be suited and ready, their gas jets programmed to take them down to airlocks. The passengers themselves would need no skill or experience, so long as Burton and his crew could keep them calm and stop them doing anything foolish. It would take a while to cycle eight hundred people through the ten suitable airlocks—but that was just a question of patience. Their suits could keep them alive on the surface for a hundred times longer than they'd need.

Anna stared at the projections in front of her, at the orderly succession of eight hundred hair-thin trajectories splitting from the *Arcas's* circle like a strange spider's web. She'd come so close to turning these people away. But it was her job to go and face them now, to greet them as they entered, however much shame and confusion was still clamouring in her head.

She made her way down the corridors slowly; there was no hurry, no need to glide. She thought about the joy she'd seen on Olivier's face at the prospect of meeting Gustave again. Chloe had accused her of seeking a new family, but was there anything so terrible about that? She couldn't understand what Olivier had been through, but she could still stand beside him and be glad that he was safe, that his comrades were safe, and that in time even Camille would be with him. She would never stop loving Sasha, but—

"The evacuation has started," her Assistant informed her. Anna paused and stood in the corridor, watching an overlay from the port's radar. Reality was recapitulating the projection, unfurling the same beautiful web.

"Incoming call from the *Scylla*."

Anna was surprised; she hadn't been expecting a reply until the *Arcas* was in a million pieces.

"I'll take it," she said.

Vieira appeared. Anna couldn't read his face, but he did not look triumphant at his victory.

"So you've made your choice," he said. "Over."

"Yes. The *Arcas* is in orbit. There'll be no docking. Over."

"We can see everything," he said flatly. "You're taking the people out. You're sheltering the criminals. Over."

"That's not true!" Anna protested. "Over."

"What were you thinking?" he chided her. "We're not so far away that we can't image a spacesuit. The count so far is…thirty seven. Over."

Anna's overlay put the number at thirty nine—but he had to be watching, not guessing. Burton must have known that this would happen. Maybe he'd considered—for a second or two—the logistics of trying to perform the evacuation in such a way that every passenger remained hidden from the *Scylla* behind Ceres, but quickly realised that that would be impossible.

Vieira broke the silence. "You did not comply with our request," he declared. "So I regret that we can not comply with yours. *Scylla* to Ceres, over and out."

15

ANNA watched the feed from the surveyor robot as the pale speck of the cargo block emerged from the background of stars. The remnants of the life support pod had been spotted from fifty thousand kilometres, leaving no doubt as to the fate of the occupant, but the identification itself could not be completed from afar.

Thin shards of white plastic and darker composites embedded in the sheath were spread out in the familiar burst pattern of fractured elliptical rings. The robot homed in on a point a metre or so from the centre, relying on the fleet's cumulative experience of the most likely place to find tissue samples. Anna spotted a small patch of shiny grey flakes just as the image processing software flagged it for investigation. Given the time lag it was rare for her to be able to contribute to the search, but it was worth having someone looking over the robots' shoulders to help them out on those rare occasions when their own strategies failed.

The flakes proved to be exactly what she'd guessed, and the preparation and sequencing was complete in half an hour. There was a single, unambiguous match in the kinship marker database: Thierry Rocault, twenty-nine. Backing up the DNA evidence, Rocault's date of departure from Vesta was consistent with the current location of the block.

Anna passed the record on to the team's chief forensic pathologist, to be verified before the notification went out to the family. Then she shut off the overlay and swayed for a moment, fighting down panic.

When the doorbell rang she glanced at the time; more than two hours had passed, but she had no idea what she'd been doing. She looked through the security camera.

Olivier said, "I'm going to stand here until you let me in."

The last time Anna had called his bluff he'd stayed there for hours. She opened the door and stood aside.

Olivier walked over to the couch and sat down. "I'd like you to come to the wake."

"No."

"It's up to you. But I want you to be there."

"I can't. It would be an insult to all of her friends."

"None of them see it that way," he replied. "Trust me, if it was going to be like that I wouldn't put you through it."

Anna shook her head. "I can't."

Olivier said, "I've persuaded three more people to drop their actions. That still leaves seven, but I'm going to keep trying. They're just lashing out because they can't get the Vestans in front of a court yet, but everyone who's actually been willing to talk to me ends up admitting that a judgement against you would bring them no satisfaction."

"They have their rights," Anna replied. "You shouldn't try to stop them."

"Their rights?" Olivier grimaced. "The only thing they'd achieve if they won their case would be to make Ceres more vulnerable to extortion in the future."

Anna said, "We have a special name, here, for a certain kind of failure to defer to the greater good—for putting a personal sense of doing right above any objective measure of the outcome. It's called 'moral vanity'. On Ceres, it's about the worst thing you can be accused of. So I'd say that those plaintiffs stand a very good chance of success."

"And you really want to be made an example of? You want other people to be afraid to do what you did?"

Anna couldn't answer that. "What did I do? I talked myself into believing that the evacuation would go unnoticed, that I could save the *Arcas* and nothing would come of it."

"You took a risk," Olivier said firmly. "But you took the right one."

"Thousands more people died than if I hadn't. I've seen what's left of them spread across the cargo sheaths."

Olivier rose to his feet and walked over to her. "Listen to me. There's a place for algorithms that weigh up the numbers and decide everything on that basis—but if the hypocrites who accuse you of 'moral vanity' really wanted everything run that way, they should have just put their anointed algorithm in charge, and declared all their problems solved forever. If you'd turned the *Arcas* away, you wouldn't have done a greater good—you would have crushed out of existence, for yourself and everyone on Ceres, the thing that gives those numbers meaning."

Anna started sobbing. Olivier reached out and held her shoulders. "I don't know what I should have done," she said. "I don't know."

Olivier waited until she was still. "Come and say goodbye to Camille," he pleaded. "You can't sit here alone, counting bodies. Come and hear about her life."